This book belongs to

C I A R A Lisa

Beni's First Wedding

STORY AND PICTURES BY
JANE BRESKIN ZALBEN

Henry Holt and Company

· New York ·

Thank you to Rabbi Toni Shy and Rabbi Beth Davidson,
Mohini Sarna, Rathi Raja, Carey Ayres, Norma Weymouth,
Sultan Hameed, Elly Shih at the International Buddhist Society,
Pastor Charles R. Vogeley, Donna Bodossian at St. Stephen's,
Johanna Hurwitz, Christy Ottaviano, and always, Steven Zalben.

Henry Holt and Company, Inc./*Publishers since 1866*
115 West 18th Street/New York, New York 10011
Henry Holt is a registered trademark of Henry Holt and Company, Inc.

Library of Congress Cataloging-in-Publication Data
Zalben, Jane Breskin.
Beni's first wedding / story and pictures by Jane Breskin Zalben.
Summary: When a friend of the family announces that he is getting married and
asks him to be his page boy, Beni experiences his first Jewish wedding.
[1. Weddings—Fiction.   2. Jews—Fiction.   3. Judaism—Customs and practices—Fiction.]   I. Title.
PZ7.Z254Bn   1998   [E]—dc21   97-2701
ISBN 0-8050-4846-4   /   First Edition—1998

Typography by Jane Breskin Zalben
The text of this book was set in 15/19 Bembo.
The illustrations were done in gold leaf, colored pencils, and watercolor
with a triple-zero brush on Opaline Parchment.
Printed in the United States of America on acid-free paper.∞
1 3 5 7 9 10 8 6 4 2

Terms that appear in the glossary are italicized in the text.

To Steven—my beshert,
who reminds me of what's important,
and what isn't.
To this life and the next one.
L'chaim

$\mathcal{G}$randma and Grandpa shouted over the telephone
to Mama and Papa, "Uncle Izzy's getting married!
Uncle Izzy's wedding is only two months away!"
Mama giggled as she said good-bye and hung up the phone.
"Which side of the family is Uncle Izzy on?" Beni asked.
"Well," said Mama, "he's not really an uncle. He grew
up with Papa in the old neighborhood. Aunt Gertie
used to baby-sit for him. We were all very close."
"So he's almost like family?" Sara asked.
"Exactly," Mama and Papa said together.

"We want to give him the best wedding in the world. Izzy would like Beni to be the page boy," said Papa. "What's that?" Beni asked. "Do I have to turn pages?" "No," Papa explained. "You will walk down the aisle with the wedding ring." Beni felt very important. "And Sashi, Uncle Izzy's fiancée, wants Sara to be the flower girl," Mama added. Sara smiled proudly. "I know what that is. I'll carry a basket of flowers down the aisle and toss rose petals."

A few weeks later, Mama and Papa took Beni and Sara
to Morris's Clothing Store to try on different outfits
for the wedding. Mama kept saying, "They're gorgeous!"
Sara got a fancy pink dress and shiny shoes to match.
Beni got a brand-new striped black suit and *yarmulke*.
Papa bought a *tallis* embroidered with gold as a gift for Izzy.
Mama got crinoline and silk ribbons. Beni and Sara
couldn't wait for Uncle Izzy's wedding day to arrive.

Finally, it was just a week away. Mama took Beni
and Sara around the corner to Sadie's Sweet Shop.
They got pastel-colored mints. "We're going to make
little crinoline bundles filled with candy," said Mama.
"We'll tie each end with silk ribbons and throw them at Izzy
and Sashi up on the *bimah* at the *aufruf*!" Mama gleamed.
"Max is going to love that," Sara shook her head. Mama
laughed. Even Mama knew how Cousin Max could get.

The *Shabbat* before the wedding, everyone went to the synagogue for an aufruf. The bride and groom were called to the *Torah* to say prayers in honor of their wedding. There was a nice *Kiddush* luncheon afterward. Everyone at the congregation was invited. Aunt Rivka made her noodle *kugel* and *kasha varnishkas.*

"I'm going to bring the ring to the bride and groom,"
Beni said to Max as they were waiting at the punchbowl.
"Who cares?" Max said as he crunched on ice cubes
and threw several rubber spiders in the punchbowl.
"Max cares, that's who," Sara whispered to Beni.
"Grandma calls him a *vilde chaya*! A wild animal!"

On the big day, Beni and Sara were excited and
very nervous. Beni was the most scared of all.
Right before the wedding, Beni saw Izzy and Sashi
walking with Rabbi Bearstein, Cantor Blum, and Papa.
"Where are they going?" Beni and Sara asked Mama.
"Into the rabbi's study," Mama explained, "to sign a
ketubah. Now they're really married. The ceremony is
just for fun." Uncle Izzy and Sashi looked very happy
when they came out.

Then everyone heard music coming from the synagogue.
First, all the bridesmaids and ushers walked down the
aisle. Then Sara followed and sprinkled flowers.
When it was Beni's turn, he took a deep breath,
started walking, and looked straight ahead.

"Isn't Beni cute!" Aunt Gertie called out, "*Sheyna kup*!" As Beni turned to see who it was, the little velvet pillow tipped and off rolled the ring! "Oops!" Beni shouted as it tumbled under the pews. Beni got a lump in his throat and felt as if he were going to cry.

Suddenly, the music stopped. Everyone was searching for the ring. "I found it!" yelled Max, waving the ring. Beni sighed. Then he quietly asked Uncle Izzy,

"Could Max walk with me this time?" "Of course!"
Uncle Izzy said as he put his arms around Beni. So
Beni and Max went down the aisle together with the ring.

Uncle Izzy walked under the *chuppa* in the front of the synagogue. Everyone turned around, anxiously waiting to see the bride. "Aah," and "Ooh," they said when Sashi came down the aisle. "So beautiful," Bubbe whispered. Uncle Izzy walked down the steps to take his bride from her parents. Then the family stood under the chuppa. Izzy and Sashi sipped wine from a Kiddush cup after the Rabbi said a blessing. Sashi walked around Izzy seven times. And Uncle Izzy placed the ring on Sashi's forefinger. Finally, the rabbi wrapped a glass in a cloth napkin and Uncle Izzy stomped on the glass and broke it. Then he lifted Sashi's veil and gave her a great big kiss. Everyone sang out, "*Mazel tov!*" Max shouted, "Yuck!"

Papa said the *brachas* over the wine and *challah*. After he recited the prayers, he lifted his glass and made a toast. "To Izzy and Sashi, a long and happy life together!" Everyone shouted, "*L'chaim*—to life!" and the family and friends gathered in a large circle and held hands. "Let's do a *hora*!" shouted Grandma and Grandpa. Uncle Izzy and Sashi were each on a chair held high in the air by Papa and all of Izzy and Sashi's friends.

While the grown-ups danced and sang, ate and told jokes,
the cousins ran around eating little potato *knishes* and
baby franks-in-blankets until they were very very full.
Max ate so much *rugelach* he burst his buttons.
"This is the best wedding I've ever been to," Max said.
"This is the only wedding I've ever been to," Beni said.
"But I hope it's not my last!" he added.
"Me too!" Max panted. And then he and Beni fell asleep.

MAMA'S HONEY WEDDING CAKE

Sashi thought it would be heimish *(more homey, warmer) to have Mama make her famous recipe instead of buying a store-bought wedding cake from a fancy-schmancy caterer. Mama was very flattered. "Maybe it doesn't look so perfect," she said—the icing was a little lopsided—"but a gift from the heart is something more special." Sashi and Uncle Izzy added, "And that's what really counts!"*

3 cups sifted flour
1 teaspoon baking soda
1 teaspoon baking powder
3 large eggs, separated
1 cup sugar
$\frac{1}{4}$ cup vegetable oil
juice of one lemon
1 cup honey

1 cup strong coffee (brewed
   or instant)
1 teaspoon maple syrup
1 teaspoon ginger
1 teaspoon cinnamon
1 teaspoon allspice
1 teaspoon cream of tartar
1 tablespoon grated almonds

1. Preheat oven to 350 degrees.
2. In a large bowl, sift flour, baking soda, and baking powder.
3. In another large bowl, beat egg yolks and sugar until foamy. Add oil, lemon juice, honey, coffee, and maple syrup. Mix.
4. Add spices to mixture.
5. In a separate bowl, beat egg whites with cream of tartar until stiff peaks form. (Make sure beaters are clean or stiff peaks won't form.)
6. Fold egg whites into batter with a spatula. Add grated almonds, folding gently.

7. Grease two 9-inch round layer pans that are $1\frac{1}{2}$ inches deep and one 10-inch round layer pan that is $1\frac{1}{2}$ inches deep.
8. Pour batter two-thirds full to allow cake to double in height.
9. Bake for 25 to 30 minutes.

Yield: 3 round cakes

Note: The more layers you make, the taller the cake will be. You can use different size pans to create a tower effect. Mama sometimes gets nutty and makes each layer a different kind of cake—chocolate, lemon-poppy, carrot, and so on!

VANILLA FROSTING

Any kind of frosting can be used between the cake layers. Mama likes a simple vanilla icing.

8 ounces softened cream cheese
1 stick of unsalted butter, softened
1 pound of confectioners' sugar, sifted
2 teaspoons vanilla
$\frac{1}{2}$ cup raisins
$\frac{1}{2}$ cup toasted pecans

1. In a large bowl, blend cream cheese and butter with electric mixer.
2. Add sugar and vanilla to mixture.
3. Fold in raisins and pecans.

Yield: 2 to 3 round cakes

GLOSSARY

Aufruf (UFF-*ruff*): Yiddish for "call up." The custom of honoring the groom by calling him up to the bimah for the first *aliyah*—the first blessings recited before and after the reading of the Torah at the synagogue service on the Sabbath preceding the wedding. Some congregations honor the bride this way as well. Tiny bags of nuts, raisins, or candies are gently thrown at the couple as they leave the bimah.

Bimah (BEE-*mah*): platform in the synagogue from which prayers are led.

Brachas (BRAH-*chahs*): blessings that always contain the words "Blessed are You, O Lord." (The *ch* in Hebrew and Yiddish is a guttural sound, like in Bach.)

Challah (CHAL-*lah*): an egg-rich, braided bread usually eaten on Sabbaths and at festivals.

Chuppa (CHOOP-*a*): a canopy supported by four poles under which the wedding takes place. In ancient times, the chuppa was woven with branches cut from trees that had been planted to celebrate the births of the bride and groom.

Hora (HOE-*ra*): a circle folk dance.

Kasha varnishkas (KA-*sha* VARN-*ish-kas*): buckwheat grains sautéed with onions in oil and mixed with bowtie-shaped noodles.

Ketubah (*Keh*-TOO-*ba*): a legal marriage contract, often illuminated (decorated).

Kiddush (*Kid*-DOOSH): a blessing. A Kiddush cup is a special wine cup held while a blessing is recited.

Knishes (*Kuh*-NISH-*es*): folded square or round baked turnovers filled with potatoes, kasha, spinach, or chopped liver.

Kugel (KOO-*gul*): a noodle or potato pudding.

L'chaim (*La*-CHI-*em*): Hebrew for "to life."

Mazel tov (MA-*zul tuv*): Hebrew for "good luck."

Rugelach (RUG-*a-lach*): rolled pastries made with cinnamon, raisins, nuts, and jam.

Shabbat (*Sha*-BAHT): Jewish Sabbath, observed from sundown on Friday until the first three stars appear in the evening sky on Saturday, approximately one hour after sundown.

Sheyna kup (SHAY-*na kup*): Yiddish for "handsome" or "pretty" (literally: "beautiful head").

Tallis (TAL-*is*), or Tallit (*Ta*-LEET): a prayer shawl.

Torah (TOE-*ra*): the first five books of the Bible.

Vilde chaya (VIL-*da* CHI-*ya,* with the Scottish *ch* of *loch*): Yiddish for "wild animal."

Yarmulke (YAH-*mal-ka*): skullcap (or beanie) to cover head.

RELIGIOUS WEDDING CUSTOMS

JUDAISM

Before the ceremony, a Jewish couple signs a *ketubah,* a Jewish wedding contract, in front of the rabbi and two witnesses. Some Jews also observe the custom of lifting the bride's veil so that the groom can make sure he is marrying the right bride! This custom dates to ancient times. In the story of Jacob, Jacob loved Rachel and asked her father for her hand in marriage. Rachel's father agreed, but tricked Jacob and gave him a veiled bride—Rachel's older sister, Leah.

The couple gets married under a *chuppa.* The bride's and groom's parents stand alongside them. A chuppa can be an embroidered ceremonial cloth, a *tallit,* or flowers. This canopy is symbolic of the home the couple will build together.

The groom places a simple gold wedding band on the bride's right-hand forefinger. It is believed that the vein in that finger goes directly to the heart. The bride's acceptance is referred to as *kiddushin* (sanctification).

In some religious services, the bride circles the groom seven times. This represents many ideas: the creation of a new family circle, a wall created to keep out evil spirits, and a way for the bride to enter the groom's *s'ferot*—the spheres of his soul. The Talmud mentions only six wedding blessings, but since the sixth century, *Kiddush* has been added to make the number seven, which is considered a mystical number in Judaism.

Breaking the glass takes place at the end of the ceremony. The groom crushes the glass wrapped in a cloth napkin with his right foot. It symbolizes the fragility of life and, to many, the destruction of the Temple. The act reminds everyone that life has both pain and joy.

CHRISTIANITY

Christians are wed by a minister or priest. Often the couple select scriptures, psalms, hymns, or poems read by family or friends. The Gospel is read by the priest. The wedding band is placed on the third finger of the bride's left hand. In a double-ring ceremony, the couple exchange rings. The rings, blessed by the priest, represent the eternity of God. Vows are exchanged. Sometimes the bride and groom each take a lit candle and light a *unity candle* to symbolize that the two shall become one. If they take *communion,* the couple will drink from the same cup of wine. This act symbolizes the life they will share together. Christians regard marriage as a rite or religious sacrament. They agree to remain together and often profess "for better or worse, for richer or poorer, in sickness and in health, until death do us part."

Tradition has it that the bride wears a white dress as a symbol of purity, and sometimes covers her face with a veil. Often, there are bridesmaids, ushers, a matron or maid of honor, and a best man present. There can also be a page boy, or ring bearer, and a flower girl. After the marriage ceremony, a reception usually follows with a feast. The bride may take her first dance with the groom, followed by a dance with her father. After dinner, the bride and groom may take turns cutting the cake and feeding one another. Sometimes the bride tosses her bouquet to eligible female friends and family. The catcher of the prized charm will supposedly be next in line for marriage.

ISLAM

Nikka, or *aqd*—a wedding contract—is signed before the ceremony so that the couple will live together according to the Muslim holy book, the Koran. Usually, an *imam,* the leader of community prayers, presents the contract to the bride and groom in front of four witnesses: two from the bride's side and two from the groom's. When marriages do not take place in a mosque they are performed by a *qādi,* a judge with four witnesses testifying to the bride's lineage. Those present pray for a happy and prosperous life for the couple and recite the *fātiḥah,* the opening chapter of the Koran.

Intricate designs are hand-painted (the powder of crushed leaves of the *mehndi* tree or a black dye is used) on the palms and soles of the bride. This custom is sometimes shared by the Hindus and Sikhs in India. In some parts of the world, before or after the ceremony, the couple parade through the street to and from the mosque with family and friends following behind. The bride is adorned with elaborate jewels and gold and a veil. Some women are veiled their entire lives, not just on their wedding day. The groom hosts the feast that follows the ceremony (called a *walīmah*). National or individual customs determine the type of celebration since Islam is practiced in many different countries and cultures.

HINDUISM

The wedding ceremony is performed by a *pujari* (a priest) in front of a sacred nuptial fire where the couple make their vows, and concludes with the *saptapadī,* or Seven Steps, which can last many hours. The bride is led around the nuptial fire in a clockwise direction, offering grains (rice) to "bring bliss." The bride and groom take seven steps in a circle around the fire. Each step represents a particular blessing: food, strength, wealth, happiness, progeny, cattle, and devotion. After the seventh step is taken, the Brahmin (high priest) sprinkles the couple with holy water and the marriage is complete. The groom then sprinkles a red powder *(sindoor)* over the part in the bride's hair. This symbolizes that they are married. The bride and groom place garlands of flowers over each other and put their right hands on each other's hearts. The groom says, "Into my heart will I take thy heart, thy mind shall follow my mind."

The groom will sometimes wear a turban called a *tupi,* decorated with jewels, feathers, or sequins, and the bride often wears bangles.

SIKHISM

Sikhs may be married by any respected religious person of the community. The "ceremony of bliss" is referred to as *Anand Karaj* and takes place in front of a special book called the *Guru Granth Sahib.* The *anand* rite must take place in the presence of this book, which the couple circle four times. As the bride and groom walk clockwise around the *Guru,* four marriage hymns *(lavan)* are sung. Wedding guests toss flower petals at the couple as musicians play between the chants. The couple show they accept their vows by bowing to this volume of teaching.

The bride wears pants *(shalwar)* and a shirt *(kameez)* in bright colors embellished with gold embroidery. A heavy veil also embroidered in gold is draped like a shawl around her head, but not covering her face. The groom wears a deep red turban and a long pink scarf as a symbol of unity with the bride. The bride and groom hold the same pink scarf, and the bride follows the groom as they circle the holy book four times.

BUDDHISM

Buddhist couples are blessed by a monk in a philosophical ceremony that is not considered religious. They promise to keep the *Five Precepts,* ethical guidelines, "training principles," or teaching ways to lead a good and happy life. These precepts are: no killing of any living things, no stealing, no alcohol, fidelity, and honesty. Marriage is a sacrament in Buddhism like in Christianity.

Buddhists can marry in a temple, often with traditional Asian music and costume. The bride wears a red gown, which symbolizes good fortune and prosperity. The groom sometimes wears a long traditional robe. In celebration, there is a big party and a vegetarian feast.

❧ Wedding Party ❧

DATE: _____

BRIDE: _____

GROOM: _____

MAID OF HONOR: _____

BEST MAN: _____

BRIDESMAIDS: _____

_____

USHERS: _____

_____

FLOWER GIRL: _____

RINGBEARER: _____